For Tess and David.

OXFORD
UNIVERSITY PRESS

Great Clarendon Street, Oxford OX2 6DP

Oxford University Press is a department of the University of Oxford.
It furthers the University's objective of excellence in research, scholarship,
and education by publishing worldwide

Oxford is a registered trade mark of Oxford University Press
in the UK and in certain other countries

Text and illustrations © Richard Byrne 2017

The moral rights of the author/illustrator have been asserted Database right
Oxford University Press (maker)

First published in 2017

British Library Cataloguing in Publication Data
Data available

ISBN: 978-0-19-274973-4 (hardback)

10 9 8 7 6 5 4 3 2 1

Printed in China

Paper used in the production of this book is a natural, recyclable product
made from wood grown in sustainable forests. The manufacturing process
conforms to the environmental regulations of the country of origin.

Visit www.richardbyrne.co.uk

The elephants were getting ready for the long march to the watering hole at the back of the book.

ELIZABETH   ELEANOR   ELTON

'Can I go first this time?'

ELGAR   ELPHIE

'Sorry, Elphie

'Hey, nobody turned up!
Wait for me!'

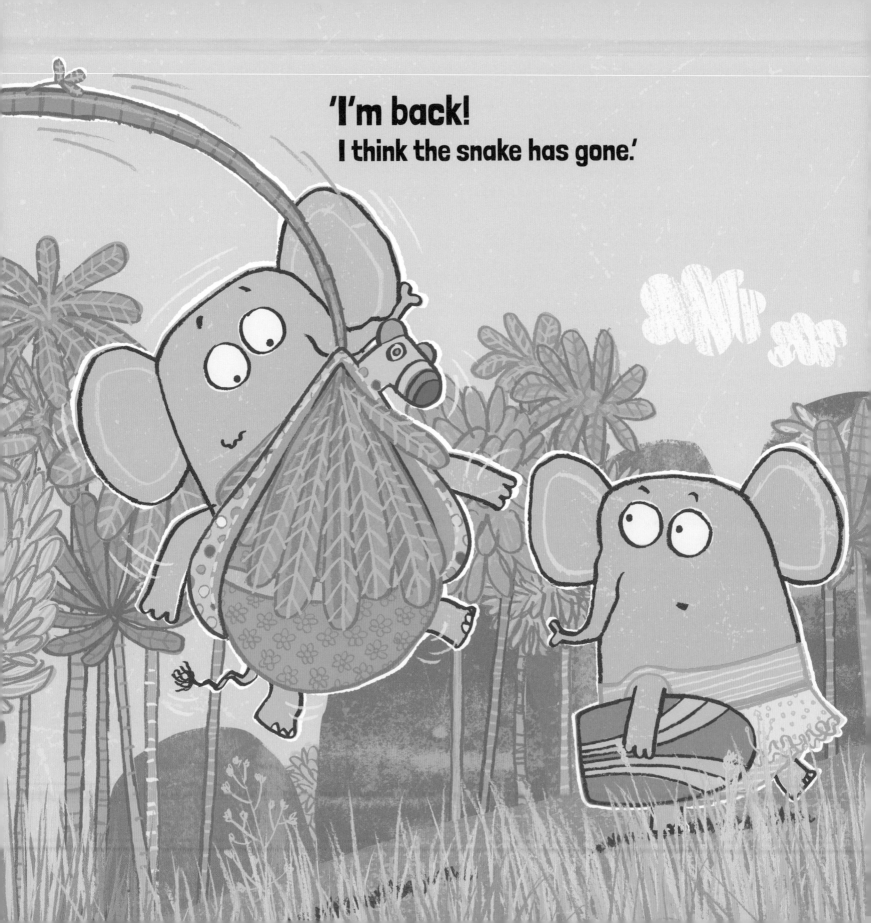

'I'm back!
I think the snake has gone.'

'After you. I'm not going on that bridge while it's so wobbly!'

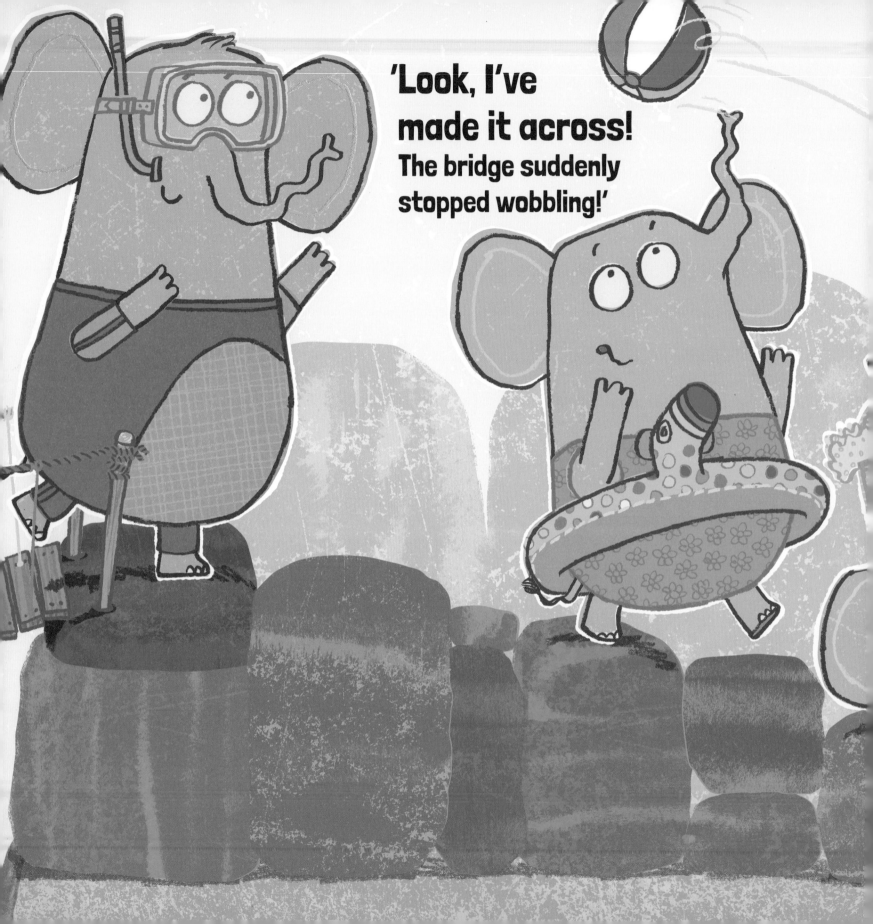

'Look, I've made it across! The bridge suddenly stopped wobbling!'

OARING!

'Elgar, **STOP!** Didn't you hear the scary mouse? Or the frightening gorilla or crocodile or lion?'

'Don't be silly, Elphie. I'm not scared of noisy . . .

'Okay, we're here so let's all get back into the right order, please.'